READ AT YOUR OWN RISK

REMY LAI

Henry Holt and Company
New York

DAY 1, MONDAY NIGHT

Once upon a time,
       I skipped assembly,
        snuck into the attic,
       awakened an evil,

          and now

          I'm h^aunted.

It was Mabel's fault.
This morning, she said,

There's nothing spooky about sitting in this hall and listening to some boring author talk about his spooky books, which I bet aren't even that spooky.

It was Brian's fault.
This morning, he said,

> You know what would ACTUALLY be spooky? Sneaking up to the attic. It's **HAUNTED.**

It was Lisa's fault.
This morning, she said,

> Let's go to the attic.

> And play a game.

> My cousin taught me. It's called...

SPIRIT OF THE COIN

It was Brian's fault. He ...

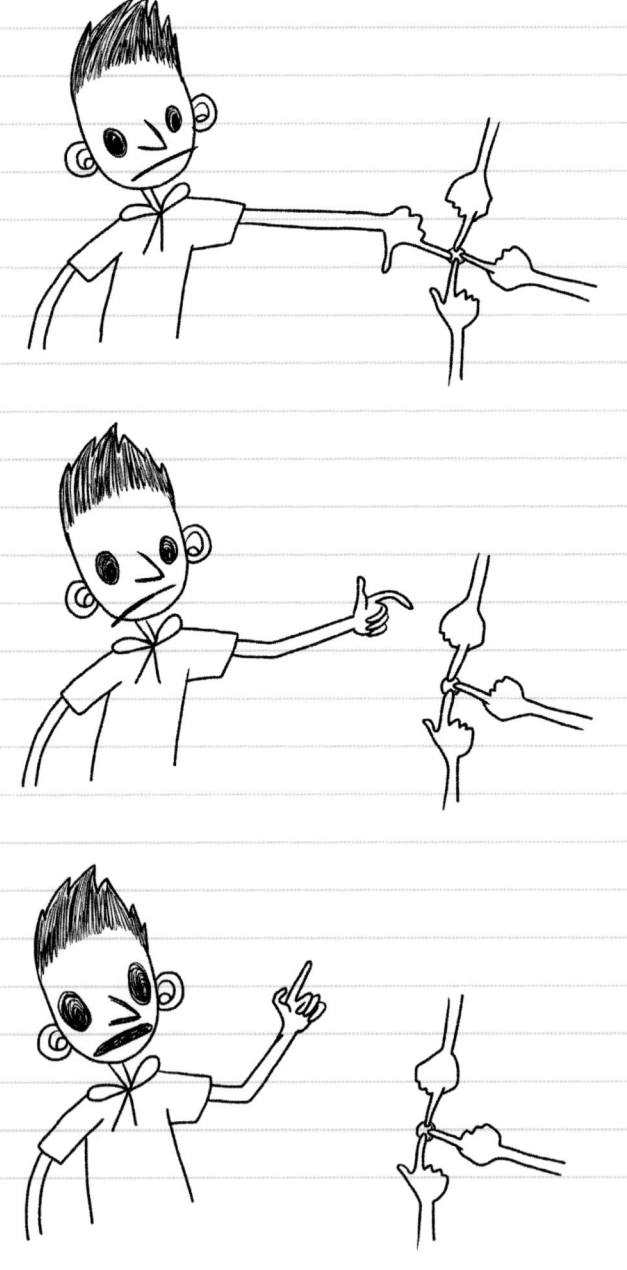

I don't want to die.

I'm only in seventh grade.
There are so many things
I haven't done.

If the words in this journal
are my last,
at least
they will shed some light on

what
 happened
 to
 me.

The first clue
that something is haunting me
came earlier this afternoon.
The bell had rung,
and all my friends had gone home,
and I was running out of school when
I felt on

my back TWO HANDS push,

then around my wrist, A HAND pulled.

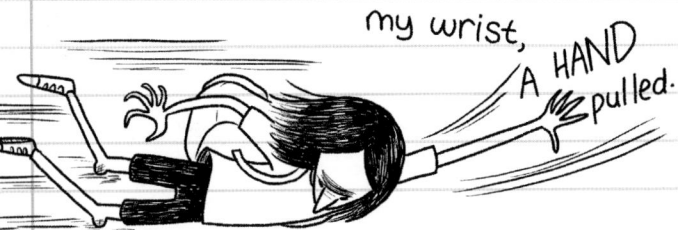

Knees against asphalt.
Gravel vs. skin.

I looked up. NO ONE was around.

I climbed out of bed, sat at my desk,
opened the first page
of a brand-new notebook.

Now, I'm still wide awake
and writing these very words,
even though I've never been
the type of kid who keeps diaries.

But

then again,

I've never been

about to
be made to

DAY 2, TUESDAY MORNING

It's lucky it's dead.

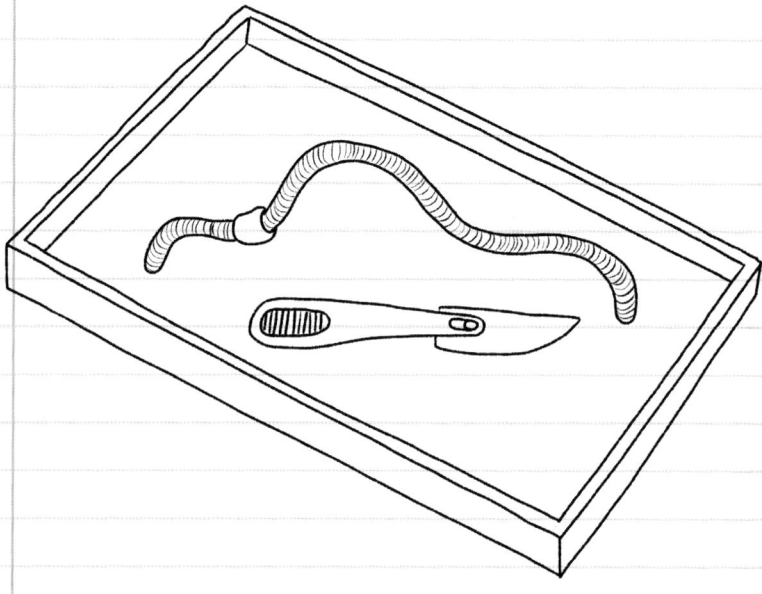

Or it would feel each slice
of Mr. Steed's blade,
all in the name of education,
for middle schoolers to discover
the things under
skin and flesh
that keep us alive.

AHEM.

I **did** want
>to attend that assembly.

I did **not** want
>to explore the attic.

Everyone knows
the library that used to be
up there was moved
because the attic is HAUNTED
>by the three students
>>who met
>>their u
n
t
i
m
e
l
y

E
 N
  D
   S

there,
under seriously
>mysterious
circumstances.

But Lisa said that up in the attic, we'd ask the SPIRIT questions:

Does Jesse like Jeremy?

Does Jeremy like Amber?

Does Jeremy like Jesse?

So I went up
because I had to know the answers,
because I think Jeremy
is nice
   and
      cute.

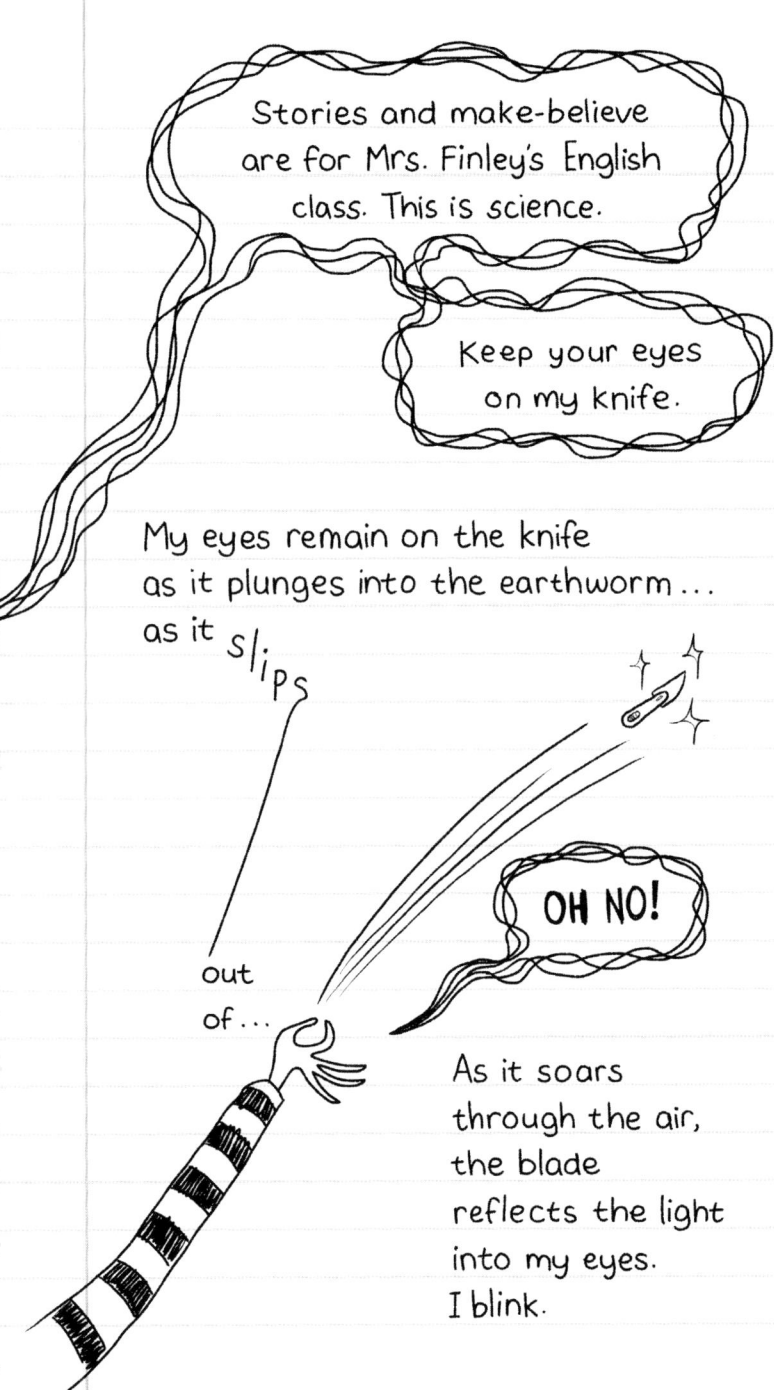

I open my eyes
to see
Brian, Mabel, and Lisa,
their eyes following
　　　the knife
　　　　as it sails through the air,
　　right for the invisible bull's-eye
　　that the curse has painted

smack-dab
in the middle

of my forehead.

DAY 2, TUESDAY AFTERNOON

Mr. Steed, Principal Tache, the ER doctor, and Mom all call it an

But I know the word for someone who goes to science class to dissect earthworms and gets sliced in the forehead by an earthworm-juice-encrusted blade and has to get two stitches:

DAY 3, WEDNESDAY MORNING

I wake up
 earlier than my alarm clock
 because my gums tickle
 on the inside.
Like there are worms crawling
                              and *SLITHERING EVERYWHERE*

I tell Mom and Dad, but
they think I'm just

OUT OF SORTS

   from my recent "accidents."

   I've got plenty of sorts.
   What I'm out of is time.

I wish
he had zipped it on Monday, too.
That morning, we snuck
out of assembly and
up into...

How to Play
SPIRIT OF THE COIN

① Draw the game board.
② Place a coin on 🏠
③ Each player places a finger on the coin.
④ Politely invite the spirit.
⑤ If the spirit accepts your invite, the coin will move.
⑥ Keep your fingers on the coin.
⑦ Ask the spirit questions.
⑧ The spirit replies by moving the coin to (YES) or (NO) or spelling out its answer.
⑨ When you're done, thank the spirit and politely instruct it to "go home."
⑩ Wait until the coin moves to 🏠
⑪ Only when the coin is on 🏠 can you remove your fingers.

Lisa pressed her index finger
onto the coin.
Mabel followed suit.
Then I did.
   But...

You three must also believe in tarot cards, astrology, and the TOOTH FAIRY.

SHUSH OR PLAY!

I wish, I wish, I wish
Brian had chosen **SHUSH**.
But he chose PLAY, and now...

Mabel and Lisa run after me.

Ignore Brian! He's ALWAYS trying to scare us!

Worms in brains! Rrright! The itch is in your gums anyway!

I see...

something...

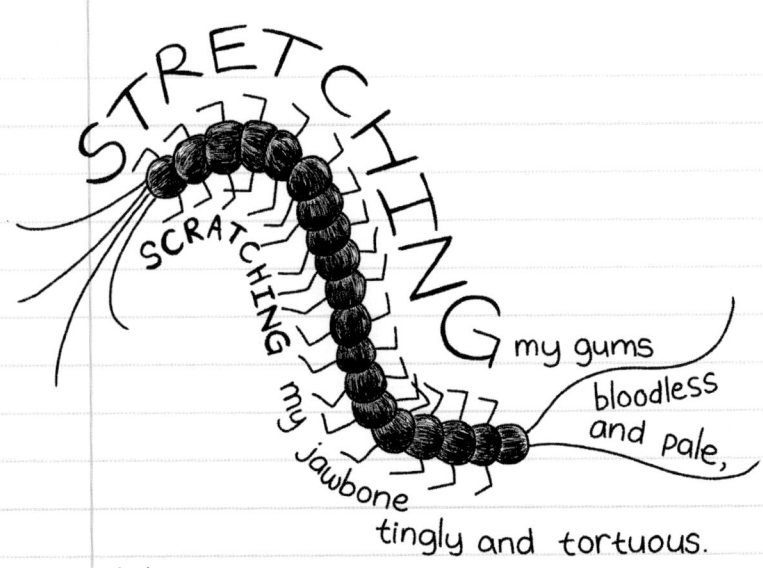

STRETCHING
SCRATCHING my jawbone
my gums
bloodless
and pale,
tingly and tortuous.

Whatever it is,
it has many legs.
Through my skin,
I see those legs crawling,
FEEL them wriggling.
Definitely not an earthworm.
At least Brian is wrong.

I show it to Mabel and Lisa,
but it disappears.

Mabel asks me why
I'm acting as if this notebook
is my cell phone, as if
my life depends on it.

What I'd give to simply be vexed
by teen feels.
Instead, I'm hexed
by ancient evil.

    No matter the price,
    I have to break this curse.

DAY 3, WEDNESDAY NOON

Ignoring the centipede wriggling
in my gums
is incredibly difficult,
but not impossible,
when I'm staring at
Jeremy's
beautiful...

handwriting.

Reading Leon Star under your desk again?
Leon Star is truly the Curse Professor! The curses in his Once Upon a Curse series just get more and more horrendous! Did you know that he graduated from our school? His favorite drink is coffee. He likes palindromes.

Words that spell the same forward and backward!

Like Hannah :) He likes semordnilaps, too.

Words that spell another word backward.

Yes. Like "evil" and "live."

Did you know that he was a great writer even when he was a kid? I read the book he wrote when he was our age.

He still lives around here.

Remember at the assembly, he told us that he often writes at that café? And that we can look for him there if we need writing advice?

What café?

The one three blocks from our school. Next to the dentist. Hey, you're BLEEDING!

What are you

Blood.

But even as the nurse blames
the dry weather,
over-vigorous nose blowing,
over-enthusiastic nose picking,
    I know
this is not something medicine
              or science
        can explain
         or solve.

So once
  the last bell RRRING

off I go
to seek
the Curse
Professor.

DAY 3, WEDNESDAY AFTERNOON

In Greek, Leon means "lion."
But Leon Star
looks like another animal.

I plop my diary on the table and my butt on the seat.

Leon Star's beady eyes dart between and

"Have you... ...come for writing advice?"

But before I can reply...

Leon Star gulps,
then asks where I was
when I first got cursed.
I tell him the attic
of Building B of our school.

The curse you're under
is one of the most <u>DANGEROUS</u>.
You do not have much time
before it ends
you.
I know of three cursed ones
who each succumbed
on the afternoon
of their eighth cursed day.

Suddenly his head snaps up,
his beady eyes pop open
as wide as marbles.

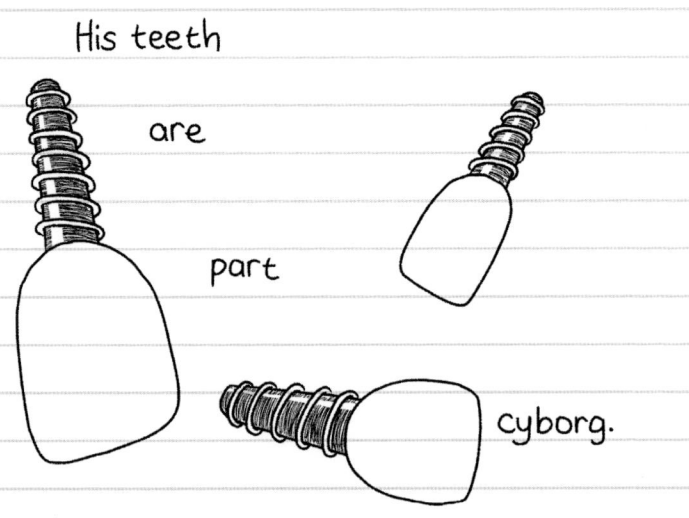

Then Leon Star bolts outside, hops into his car.

Leaving me all alone with my curse.

What a waste of perfectly good coffee.

Are... Are you the one...
who cursed me?
> What a delightful pleasure it is
> to finally meet
> > my victim.

Did... Did you spill that coffee?
> All it took was a suddenly,
> > mysteriously
> > slippery floor.

That coffee was STEAMING!
> And scalding.

As I said,
> perfectly good coffee.

And I heard
> coffee
> is his favorite drink.

WAIT! You were trying to hurt HIM?
Don't worry,
> HANNAH.
> I won't let anyone,
> > no one,
> meddle in our little game.

Why are you doing this?
Hello???
ANSWER ME!
PLEASE!!!

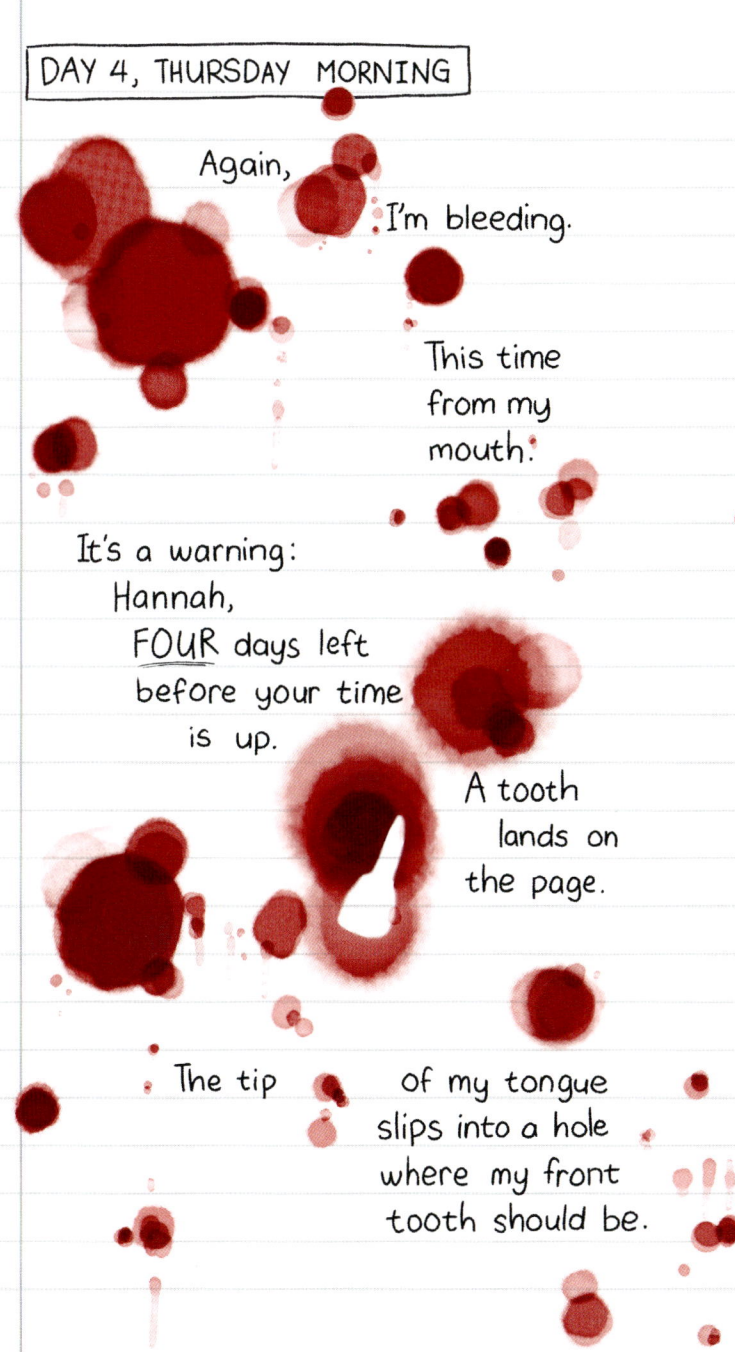

Mabel likes to exaggerate.
B- in math and her life is over.
Her crush looks at her and she faints.
But... is this the one time
she's telling it like it is?

Oh, Hannah.

Mrs. Finley's teeth
are perfect.
And she's really old, like forty.
It'd be a tragedy and so unfair
if I need dentures at my age.
So, remembering what Leon Star said,
I dash out of class
to the cafeteria
and buy a carton of milk.

Twice daily toothbrushing,
yards of minty floss,
zero decay,
zero fillings—
and now
a perfectly fine tooth
is drowning in milk.

"What **bad luck** you've been having!"

"The dentist is waiting for you."

I'm going to be TORTURED until I break the curse. Or until you meet your untimely end.

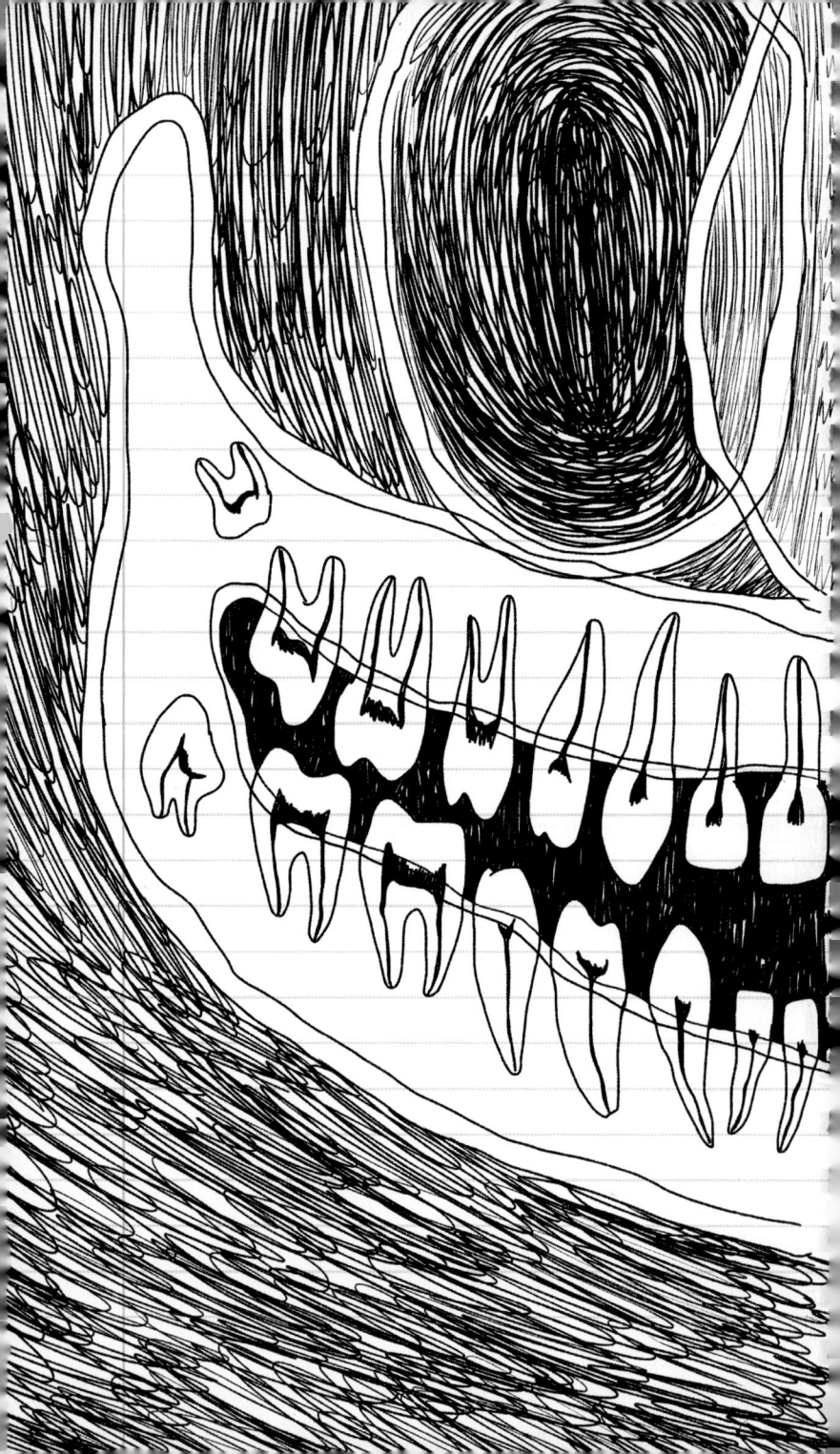

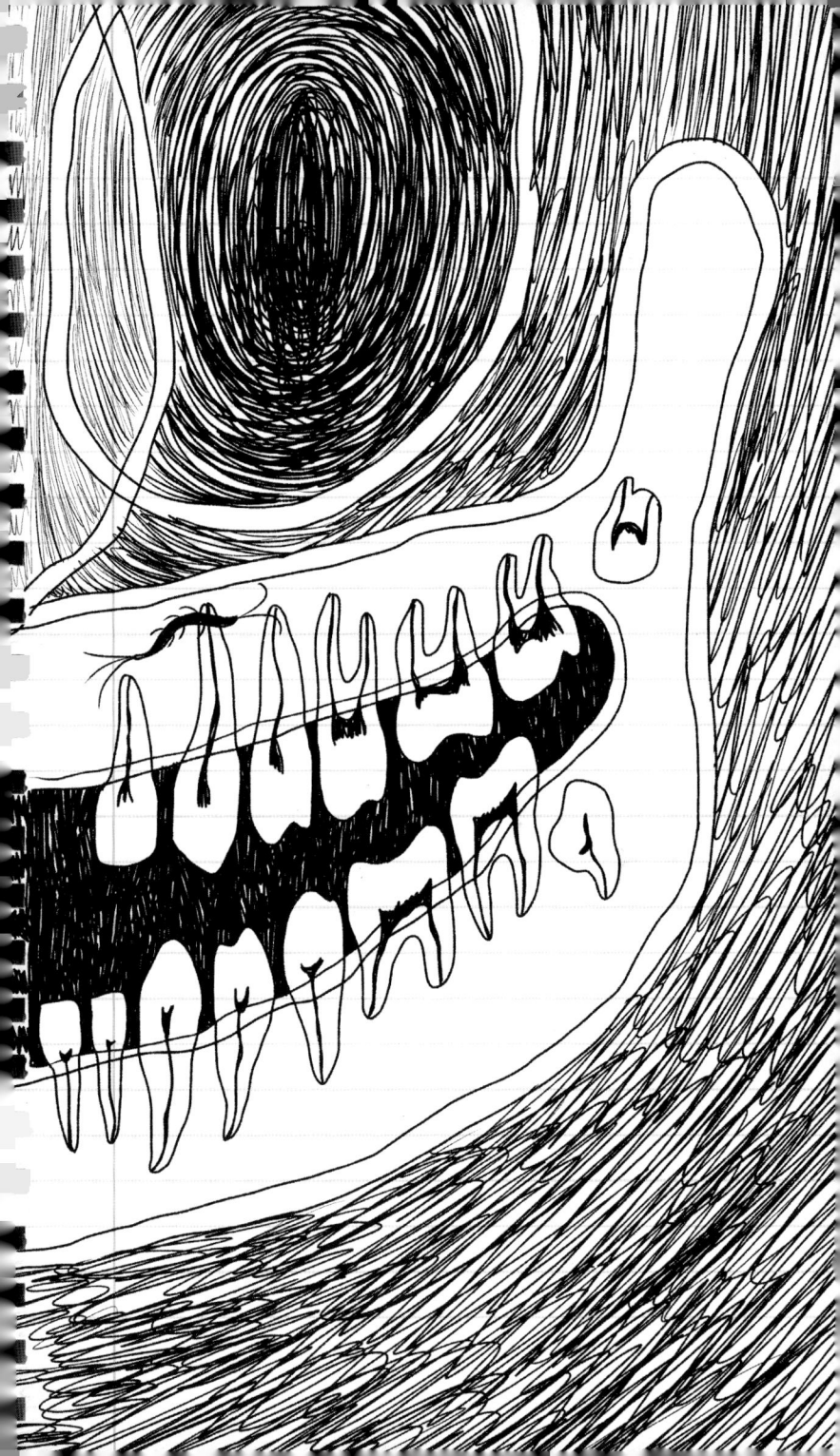

But as I leave,
I see him staring
 at the thing

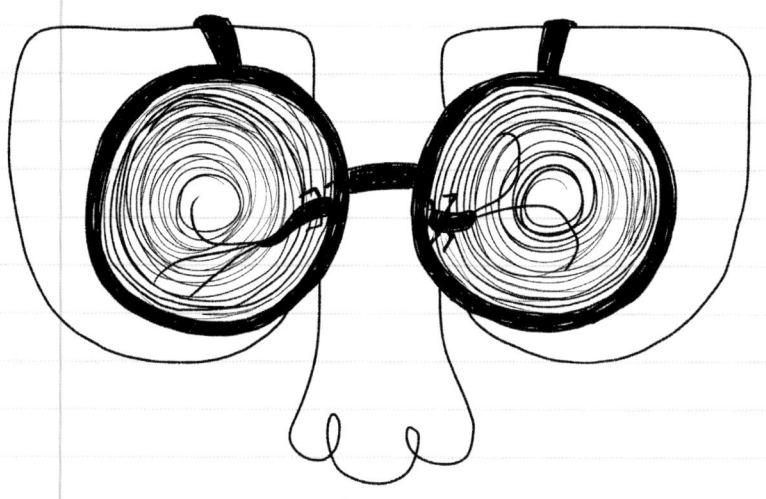

that is not real.

DAY 4, THURSDAY NIGHT

Lisa, may I talk to your cousin who told you about Spirit of the Coin?

 Hannah, are you really cursed? That's why your tooth jumped ship, isn't it?

 DROP IT, BRIAN. She's miserable enough. Stop trying to scare her!

 I'm not! I swear!

 If Hannah is really cursed, why is she the only one? We ALL played the game.

 I don't know. But the spirit chose HER from the start!

On Monday, up in that attic...

The coin slides out of 🏠

and glides to the row of letters,
first to **H**
then to **A**
then to **N**

N   A   H

BRIAN, CUT IT OUT!

You're so annoying, Brian. We know **YOU** moved that coin.

"I SWEAR I DIDN'T!"

I know it wasn't Brian.
He'd have spelled out
B-R-I-A-N-I-S-A-W-E-S-O-M-E.

I have a confession to make.
That last bit made me chuckle.
My favorite flavor
is
grim and giggles.

I shall reward you,
Hannah.

YOU'LL LET ME GO???
THANK YOU THANK
YOU THANK YOU!

You know I can't
do that. How about
a smaller wish?

May I please
keep my tooth?

ABRACADABRA.

My gums
become more and more itchy.
The centipede
is agitated, angry,
like there's a fire under it.

I can't do anything but feel its many, many legs skittering along my forehead... No! It's now scampering right under my jawbone, its feelers trailing, its body twisting and turning. Then relief comes as it becomes still —

The stitches
keeping my
forehead
together

itch

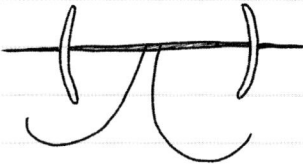

stretch

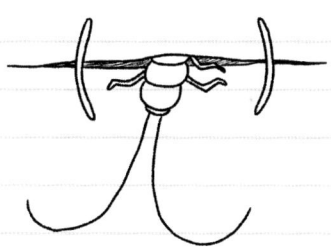

breach.

It's...

... not a centipede.

I don't know
what it is.
But I saw it
on Monday
in the attic
of Building B.

The strange bug
drops off my cheek,
scurries across the floor
and out the door.

You're welcome.

DAY 5, FRIDAY MORNING

With the bug out of me,
I can pay attention in class
and be a ~~good~~ better student.
Right now, Mrs. Finley is talking about

She tells us about an evil ruler in the folktale *The Thousand and One Nights*—how he'd been killing women because he thought they'd betray him.

The next one was to be Scheherazade.

When tomorrow came, she continued her tale.

If I tell Mrs. Finley about the curse,
she'll call it the flimsiest excuse
she ever heard
for not listening in class.

As I stammer, trying to come up
with a believable lie,
out of the blue,
my nose tickles
as if a paranormal prankster
were sprinkling invisible pepper
all over me.

I snatch my tooth off Brian's desk and dash to the cafeteria for yet another carton of milk. Aren't you sick of it yet? How about a different beverage?

YOU SAID YOU'D LET ME KEEP MY TOOTH! I'VE BEEN DOING WHAT YOU ASKED! WHY ARE YOU DOING THIS?!?

YOU'RE A LIAR!!!

You ungrateful brat.

Everyone makes such
a big deal
about the hero,

    but

what would a knight be
without monsters?
A foolish man sweating
in a tin can.

What would a vampire slayer be
without vampires?
A jobless man holding
a wooden stake.

Without the villain,

there would be no
               OBSTACLES,
      no

              OPPORTUNITIES

   for the hero to become

     a hero.

You should be grateful.
Thank you so much
for helping me to become a hero.
I will overcome this obstacle
you so kindly created for my
own good.
Please let me save my tooth.

Mom is h~~u~~angry
as she picks me up from school early
(again).
Dr. Pullman is busy torturing
another patient,
so I volunteer to go next door
and get Mom a muffin.

Leon Star is nowhere
in the café,
but the same waiter is there
with the perfectly good coffee.

Hey! Are you Hannah? Lisa's friend? I'm her cousin!

steaming
scalding

On Monday,
the one who moved the coin
and spelled out H-A-N-N-A-H
was me.

So the others wouldn't suspect me,
I yelled,

BRIAN, CUT IT OUT!

It worked.

Yeah, Brian! STOP YOUR **NONSENSE!**

Yeah! Not falling for your prank!

I only wanted to scare Brian.
Instead, I ended up
getting a taste of my own medicine.

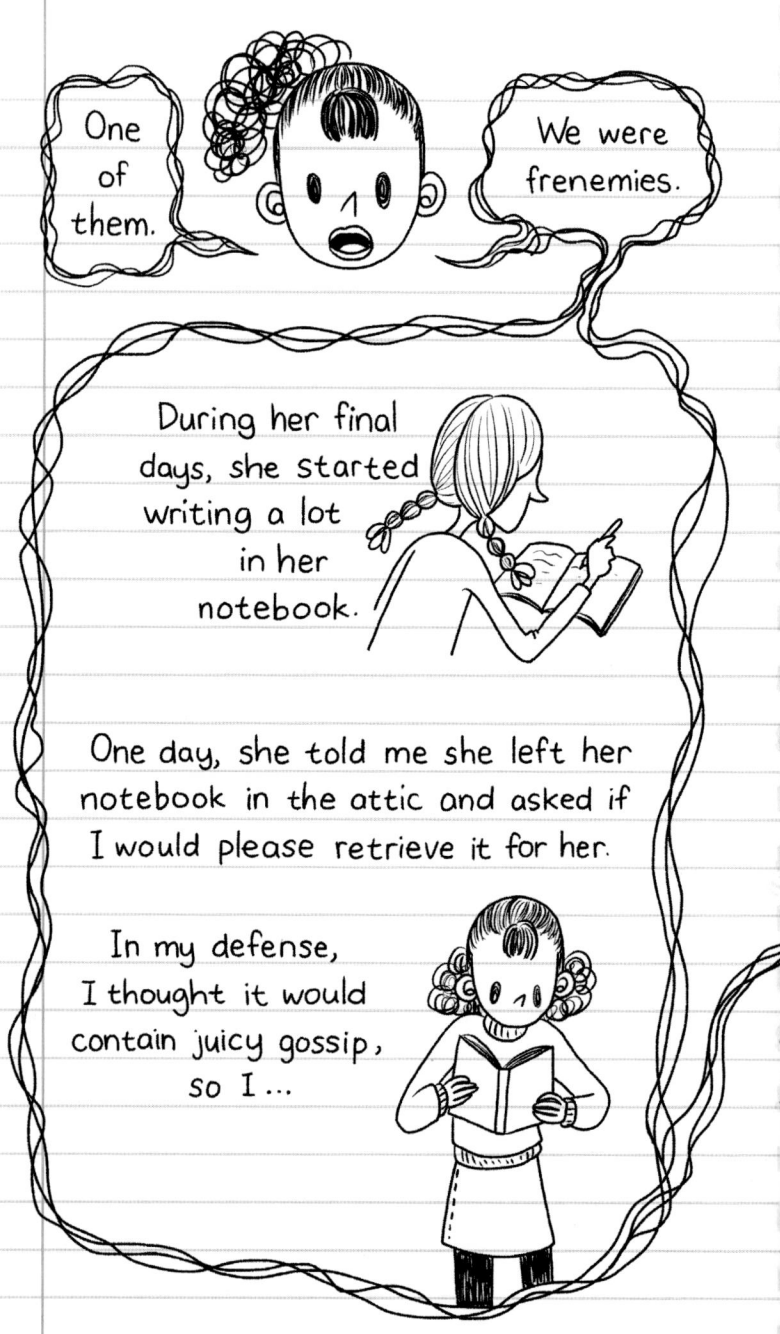

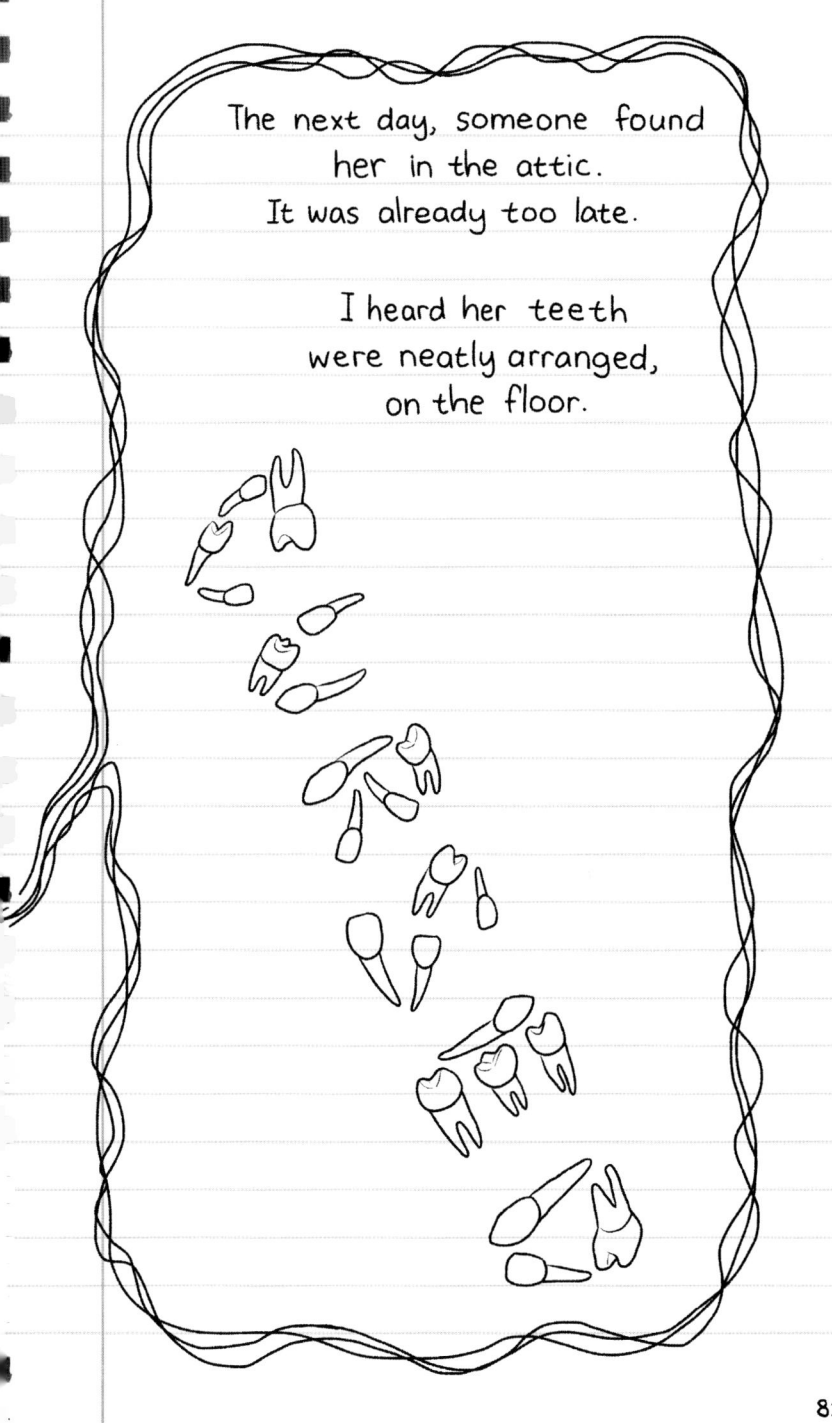

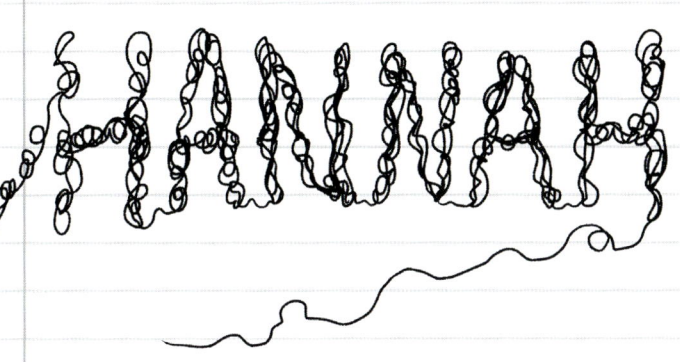

STOP IT, PLEASE!!!
LISA'S COUSIN DIDN'T DO ANYTHING! She talked too much.
PLEASE!
Oh fine. We still need her to get that muffin anyway.

While Mom nibbles on the blueberry muffin, I hand Dr. Pullman the milk.

This...

...is NOT milk.

This tooth is <u>beyond</u> saving.

Dr. Pullman glues on
a temporary fake tooth instead.
I'll have to use this plastic tooth
till I'm eighteen,
when my jawbone stops growing,
then I can get a permanent
fake tooth
made of
    metal
    and
    porcelain

SCREWED into my bone.

Mom drops me off at home
and drives away
to pick up my little brother
from school.

                I turn on the oven.

I turn the knob all the way to # MAXIMUM.

You do not want to do this, Hannah.

You said
you'd let me
keep my tooth.
I played along,
did everything
you asked.
But you lied.
I'm ending this game
              now.

HANNAH Lee
is home,
staring at the oven,
at these pages
burning
to a crisp.

    poor girl.
    How she underestimates me.
    This is not
    a game
    that is so easily
    won.

How should I make her understand
my power?
 Should I
A) Drop an anvil on her head?
B) Teleport her into a lion's cage?
C) Possess her to dance in front
    of Jeremy?
D) All of the above?

The answer is E) play a game
              with Hannah Lee's
              little brother.

All of eight years old.
Snotty nose.
Sticky fingers.
Smart mouth.

The mother
has just picked him up.
They're two blocks away.
        Hannah sighs
        with relief
        at the pile of soot
        left in the oven.

They're one block away.
        Hannah smiles
        with victory
        as she turns off
        the oven.

They're driving up the driveway.
        Hannah skips
        with the joy
        and carefreeness
        she hasn't felt
        since she met me.

Hannah watches from the window.
The mother walks
toward the house.
The brother,
for some mysterious reason,
stops in his tracks,
unzips his schoolbag,
turns it upside down,
and shakes out its contents.
Then he,
for some mysterious reason,
slowly, carefully drops
onto all fours,
rolls over onto his back,
closes his eyes,
and moves
no more.

Hannah yells, "Mom! He's fooling
          around!"
The mother yells, "Stop fooling
          around!"

    But he stays
    as still
    as a   corpse.

By the shoulders, they shake him,
but still he will not wake.
CanNOT wake.

> The mother
> bundles him into the car,
> screaming at Hannah,
> "GET BACK INSIDE
> AND CALL YOUR DAD!"

The mother's car speeds
out of sight.
Hannah stares with horror
at the brother's things
strewn all over
the driveway.

Hannah.

Hi.

I'M
SORRY!

Hi,

Hannah.

I'M SORRY I'M SORRY I'M SORRY! PLEASE DON'T KILL MY BROTHER! IT'S ALL MY FAULT! PLEASE FORGIVE ME!

You're not the first to fail to destroy the villain.

And you won't be the last.

I'M SORRY! I'VE LEARNED MY LESSON! PLEASE LET MY BROTHER GO!

Your brother is what we call "collateral damage."

NO! PLEASE! THIS ISN'T HIS FAULT!

Then is it Lisa's fault? No.

Mabel's? No.

Brian's? NO! IT'S MINE!!!

It's all my fault
that my brother
is in a mysterious coma.
Because on Monday in the attic,
after I pretended to be the SPIRIT
and spelled out H-A-N-N-A-H,
after Lisa, Mabel, and I yelled
at Brian to cut it out...

DAY 6, SATURDAY MORNING

Dad drives me to the hospital
where Mom has been since yesterday,
right next to my brother,
whose blood tests,
X-rays, brain scans
all came back normal.
But still, he hasn't moved

a leg

an arm

or a finger.

But under
his eyelids,
his eyes dart
left
    and right.

My brother is trapped
inside a body frozen in slumber.

The doctors call it a "medical mystery," but I know there is someone who can cure him.

Did you page Dr. Abracadabra?

Please let my brother wake up.

I don't work for free.

Take everything in my piggy bank!

Tsk. How disappointing. That you take me to be materialistic.

I'm sorry! I'll... pay you with a story! Or rather, a story about telling stories.

Telling a story is like piecing together a jigsaw puzzle. Only the storyteller has the box and knows what the whole picture looks like.

The storyteller deliberately chooses which piece to lay down first, next, next...

And the reader starts to see that perhaps

it's a...

pony?

The reader can't be 100 percent sure
if it's a pony
until they read to
The End,
until the storyteller
         places...

...the last piece.

At which point
the reader notices
the clues were there
all this time —
the clouds,
the rainbow.
It couldn't have been anything
but a unicorn.

> Here's another piece
> of the puzzle
> about what happened
> on Monday.

After Brian, Mabel, Lisa, and I left
the attic,
classes went on
as usual,
the last bell rang
as usual,
and I made my way
toward the exit
as usual.

> But then

I turned left and

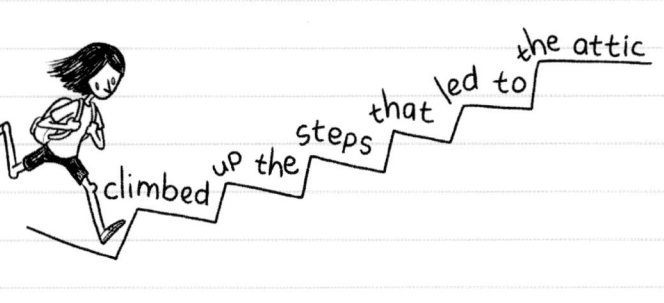
climbed up the steps that led to the attic

and then...

...I read from "Once upon a time"...

...to "The End."

And then

BONG! BONG! BONG!

DAY 6, SATURDAY AFTERNOON

The doctors call it a "medical miracle," but I know it's all thanks to Dr. Abracadabra. Aw shucks, it was nothing.

The doctors want my brother to stay for a few days longer, so they can run more tests, but I'm allowed to visit.

Last year, for class, I built a diorama, and I knew my brother would ruin it, so I placed a sign on it:

DO **NOT** TOUCH!

Well, he touched it.
　　And ruined it.

DAY 6, SATURDAY EVENING

Mabel hears
about my brother's "mishap"
from her mom, who had heard about it
from my mom.

Two minutes later,
I get the same message
from Lisa,
then Brian.

I don't reply.

Their silly chain text can't save me
from more "mishaps."

It can't save me
from whatever worse "mishaps"
will begin
on the eighth day, this coming Monday,
and will likely spell "THE END" for me,
like I've been warned.

I only have the rest of today,
  tomorrow,
 and some of Monday,
before time runs out.

> Cheer up, Hannah.
> I saved your brother, didn't I?

Thank you sooo much.

> Do I detect
>   sarcasm?

I wouldn't dare.
I'm immensely,
utterly,
eternally
grateful to you,
Oh, Your Highness.

> The father
> loves
> grapes.

While the cursed one
is at home, resigned to her end,

Why are you talking about my dad?

the father sits by the brother's
hospital bed, plucking grapes
from a well-wisher's fruit basket
and popping them whole
into his mouth.

Stop talking about my dad!

Should a grape miss
the esophagus
and instead go down
and get stuck
in his windpipe

I'M SORRY! I'M SORRY! I WON'T USE SARCASM
ANYMORE! PLEASE LEAVE MY DAD OUT
OF THIS! PLEASE!

I was just ... discouraged.

> Let me give you
> some encouragement.

Abracadabra.

Thank you so much for removing
two bugs from inside me.
I greatly appreciate
your magnanimity.
But, if you don't mind, I have
a question.

Ask away.

Wasn't there only one bug?
I only saw one on the X-ray,
and you already abracadabra-ed
that one out of me. I guess
your X-ray technology
can't detect
the eggs.

DAY 7, SUNDAY MORNING

It's all smushed and smashed,
my bowl of oats.
But I can't even eat one bite.
Not with my teeth,
all of my teeth,
   wobbling
   in their
   sockets.

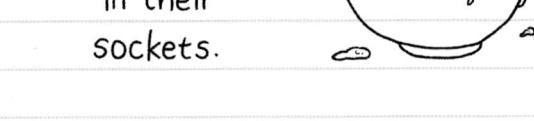

So, off we go again to Dr. Pullman.

Teeth are held in place by cementum and periodontal ligaments.

Huh?

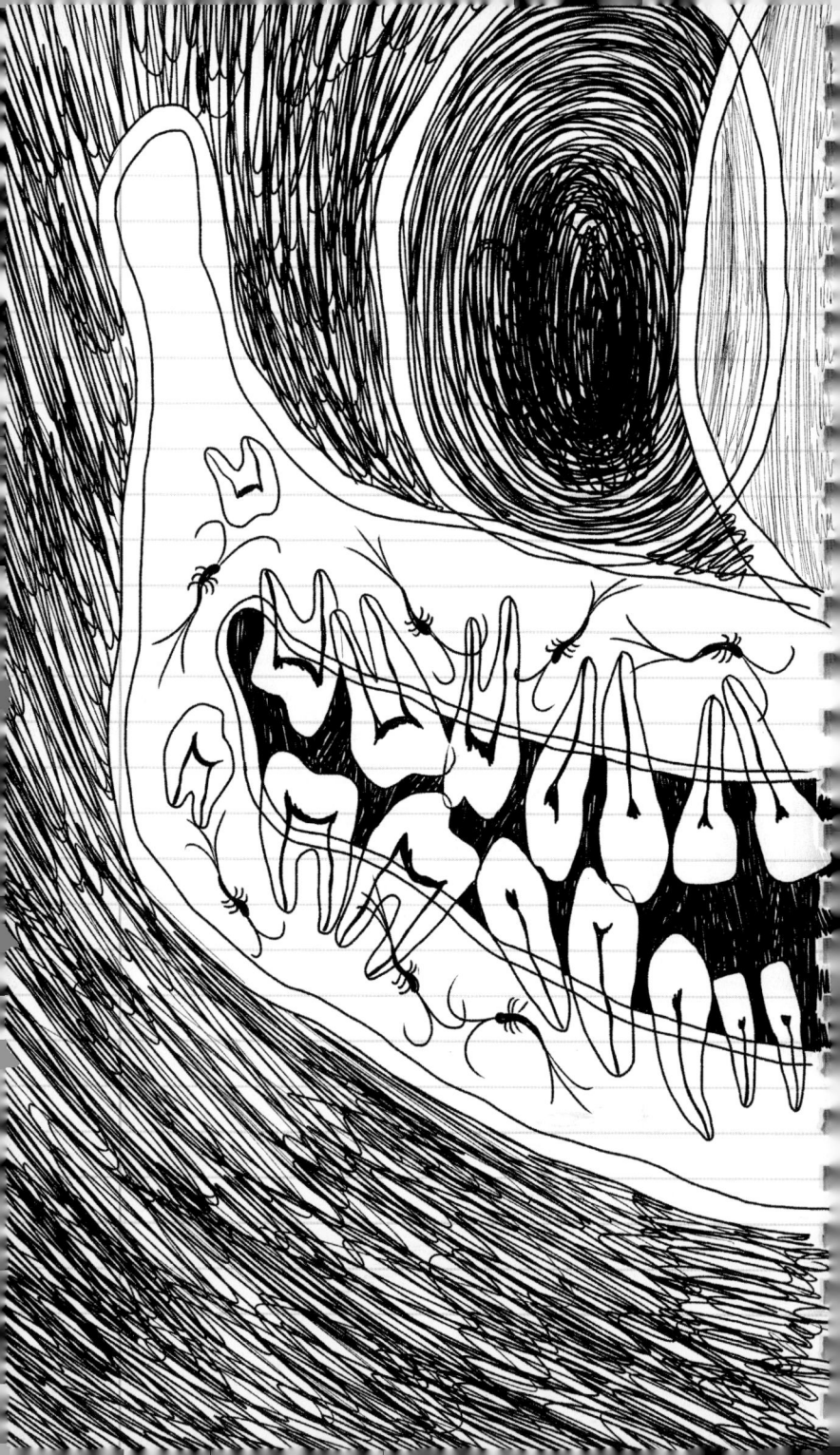

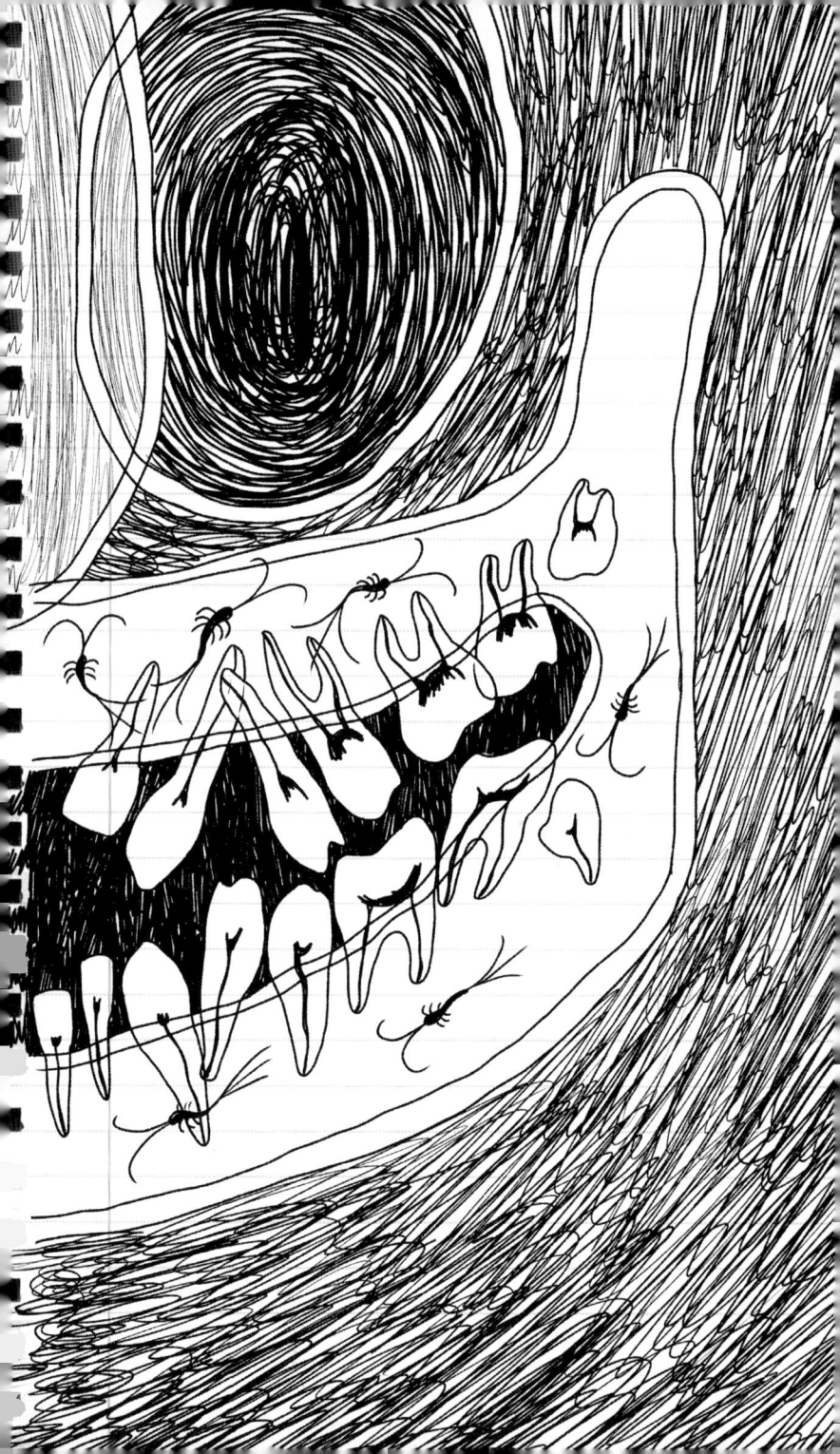

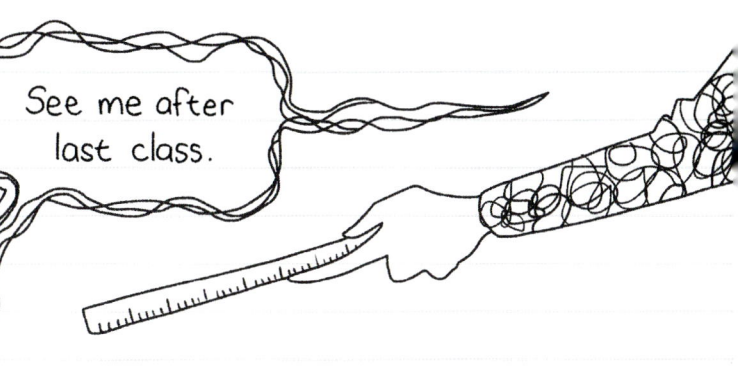

Great. My final moments will be spent listening to Mrs. Finley chew me out for not paying attention in class.

Doesn't sound like her.

How would <u>YOU</u> know?
Wait a minute.
DO YOU KNOW MRS. FINLEY?

It was a long time ago, when she wasn't yet a Mrs.

How do you know her?
Tell me. Pretty please?
I'm curious, that's all.

ANSWER ME!

But even if no one ever finds out the truth about my last breath...

... there is one truth
I want to reveal
while I still have the chance.

No, not THAT.

> Read the last page of Leon's book!

AUTHOR'S NOTE

I've been writing since I could remember. But early on, I'd get frustrated and disheartened, and I'd give up on my stories.

The first time I actually finished a story was in seventh grade.

I owe a debt of gratitude to my seventh grade teacher, who gave me tips to finish that story. She saved my life. And twenty of my teeth.

THANK YOU, MRS. FINLEY!

-Leon Star

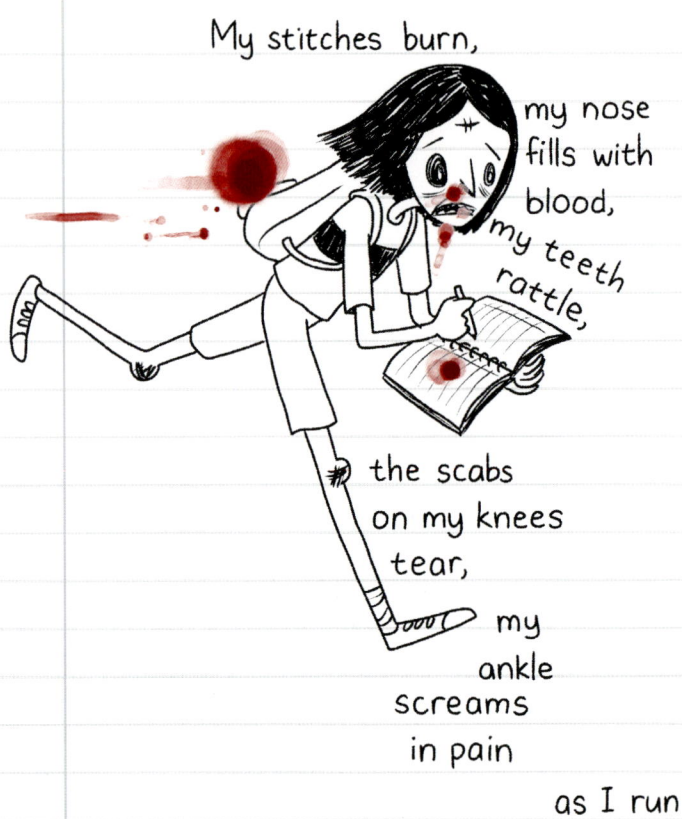

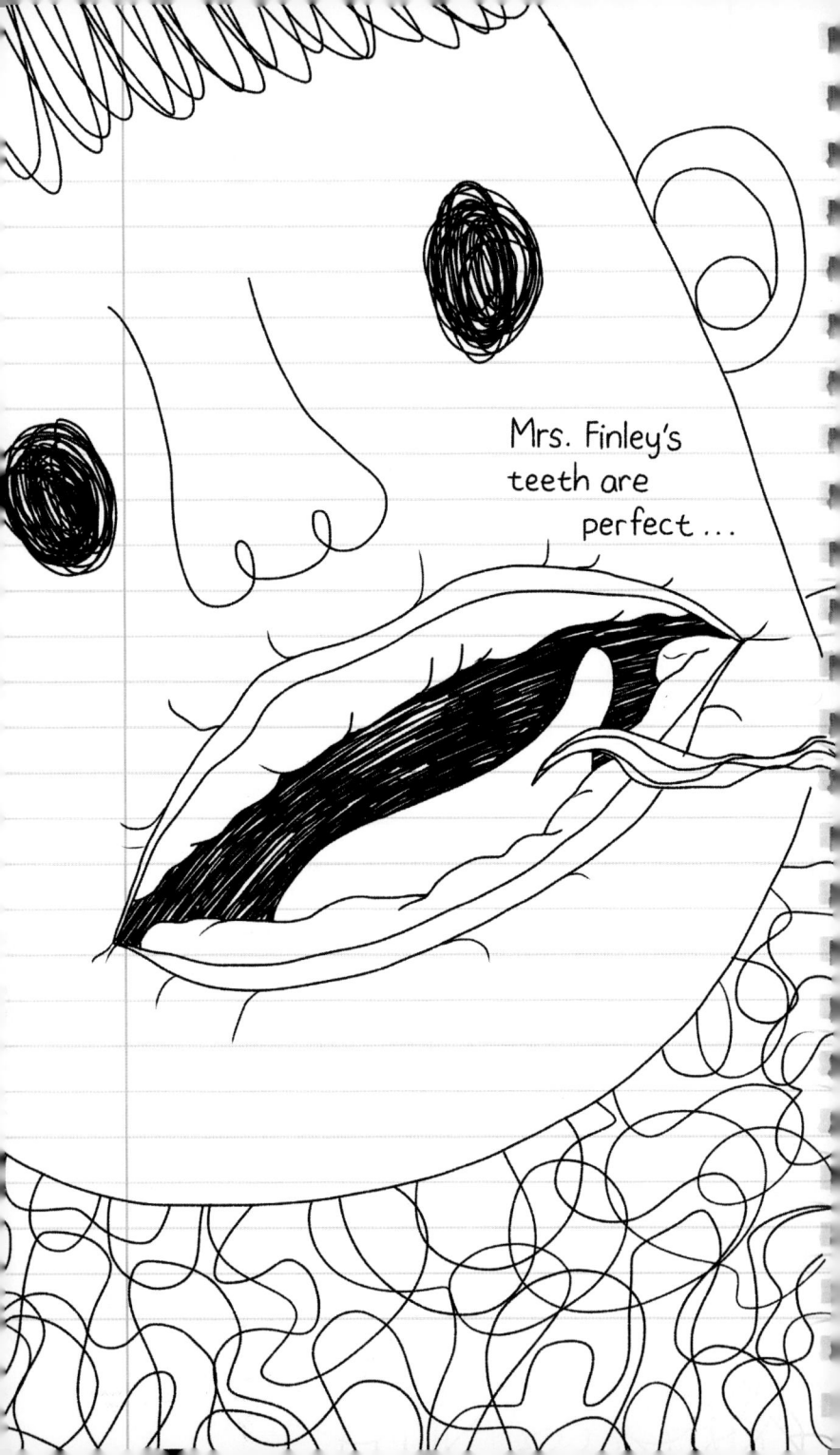

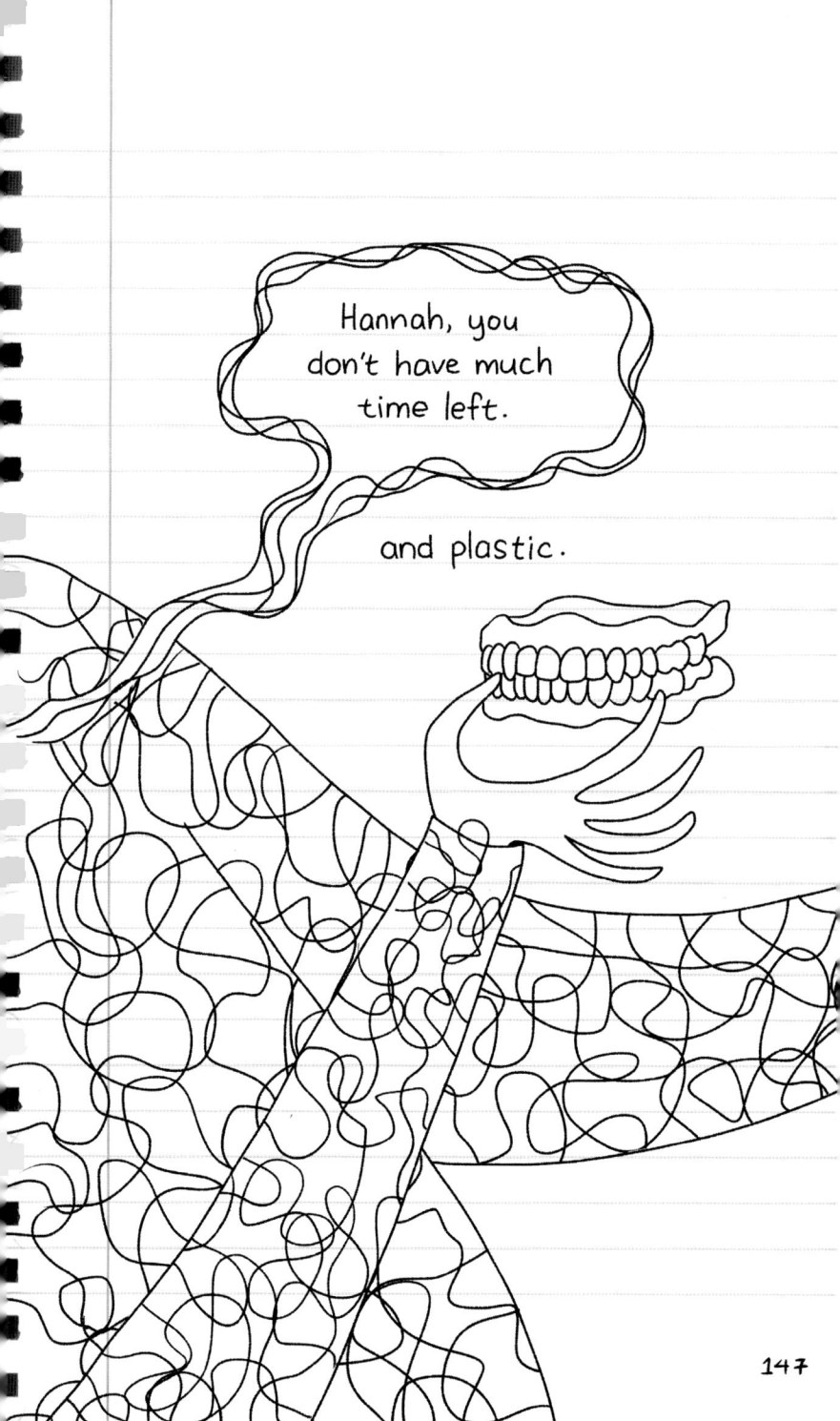

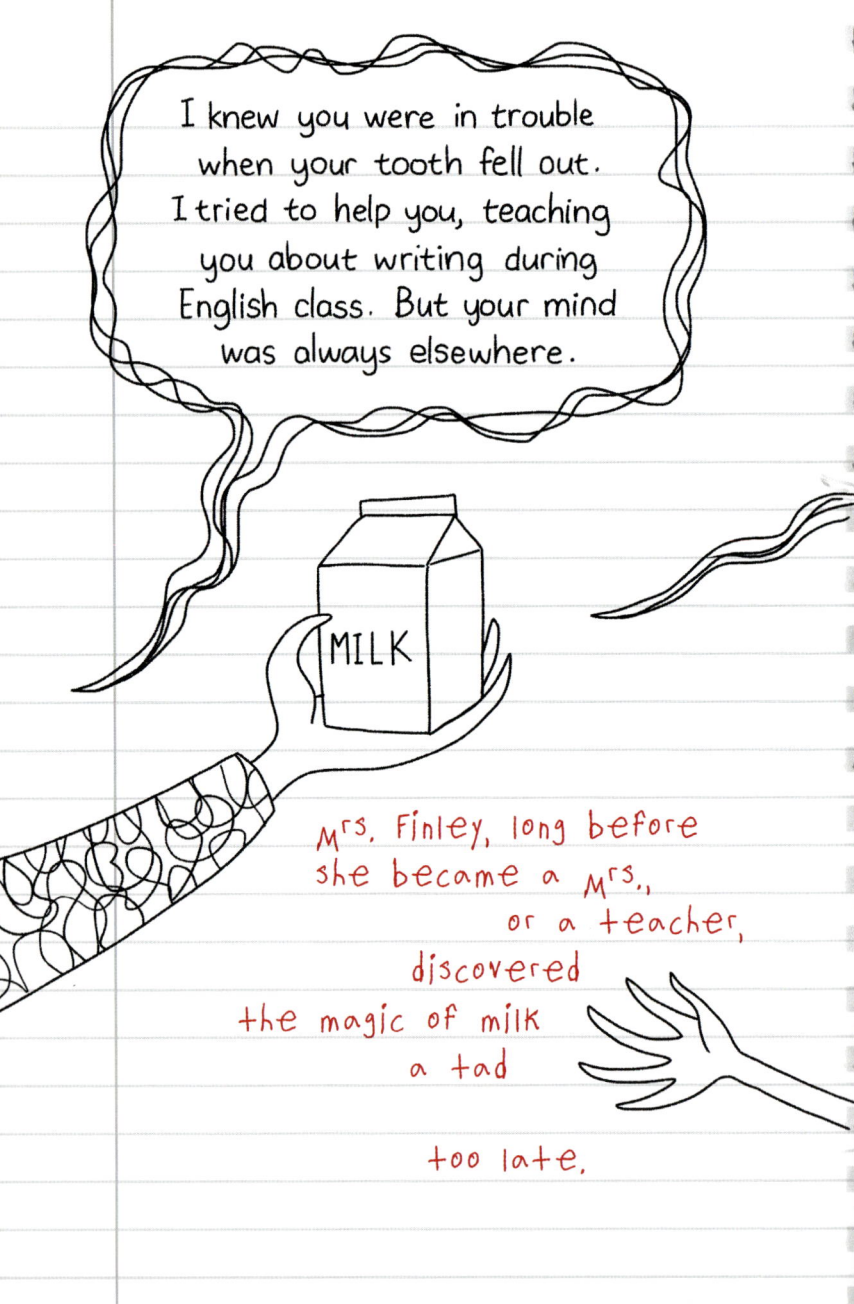

BONG!

I don't know if I will make it
to the end.
I started
this story
hoping that
at least
someone
would
find out

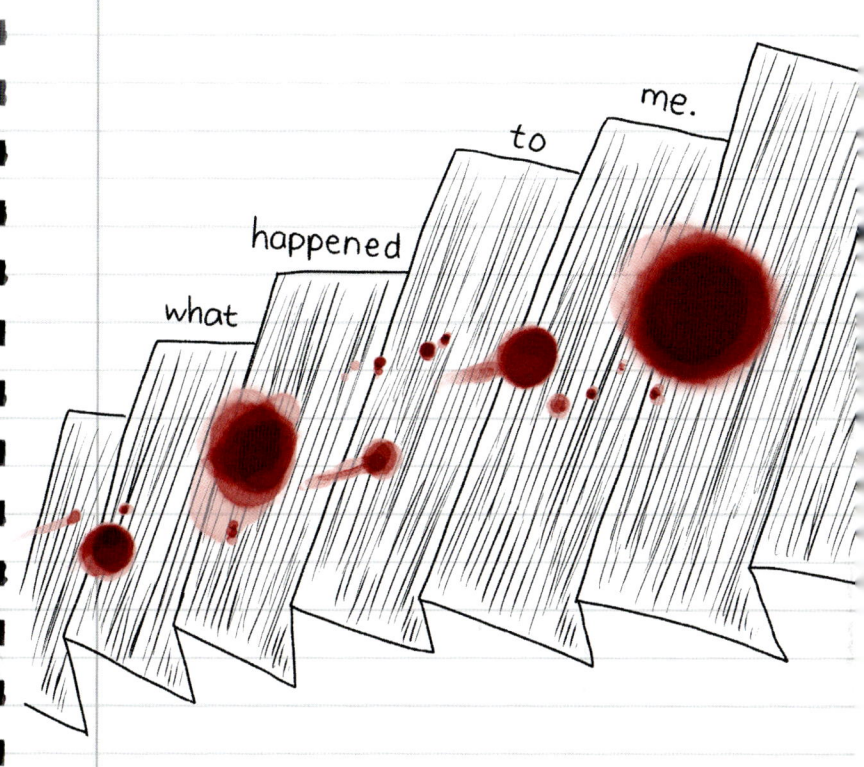

I have known
since this nightmare began,
that in order to break the curse,
there is a big price to pay.
Leon Star reminded me of that, too,
when he had yelled, "**EVIL, I DELIVER!**"
He also meant its semordnilap:
"**REVILED, I LIVE!**"

The End.

And the evil lived happily
                    ever after.

Dear Reader,
You have been cursed to suffer
unfortunate mishaps, each
progressively worse,
resulting in your untimely end.

To save yourself,
write a story that keeps
at least one reader
 reading until the eighth day,

until "The End."

Then the curse will leave you
and haunt your reader.

                    Your story starts

THANK YOU!!!

Brian Geffen

Jim McCarthy

Carina Licon

Aurora Parlagreco

Kristin Dulaney

Allene Cassagnol

Kelsey Marrujo

Samantha Sacks

Leigh Ann Higgins

Naheid Shahsamand

Elysse Villalobos

 Melissa Zar

 Mia Moran

 Ann Marie Wong

About the Author

Remy Lai lives in Australia with her two dogs, who sometimes freak her out by barking at nothing in the corners of rooms. She is also the author of the critically acclaimed Pie in the Sky, Fly on the Wall, Pawcasso, the Surviving the Wild series, and Ghost Book. Follow Remy on Instagram @rrremylai.

remylai.com

ALSO BY REMY LAI

Pie in the Sky
Fly on the Wall
Pawcasso
Surviving the Wild series
Ghost Book

Henry Holt and Company, Publishers since 1866
Henry Holt® is a registered trademark of Macmillan Publishing Group, LLC
120 Broadway, New York, NY 10271 • mackids.com

Copyright © 2024 by Remy Lai. All rights reserved.

Our books may be purchased in bulk for promotional, educational, or business use. Please contact your local bookseller or the Macmillan Corporate and Premium Sales Department at (800) 221-7945 ext. 5442 or by email at MacmillanSpecialMarkets@macmillan.com.

Library of Congress Cataloging-in-Publication Data is available.

First edition, 2024
Edited by Brian Geffen
Cover and interior book design by Aurora Parlagreco
Production editing by Mia Moran
Lettering by Remy Lai and Brian Geffen
Printed in China by RR Donnelley Asia Printing Solutions Ltd., Dongguan City, Guangdong Province

ISBN 978-1-250-32335-4
1 3 5 7 9 10 8 6 4 2